W9-ATT-735

so many cuddles

Written by Ruth Austin
Illustrated by Clare Owen

We wake up with
rise and shine cuddles,
bounding up to see
you cuddles,

and cuddles that say

I love you so,
so much.

There are grab you tightly
by the legs cuddles,
I was very scared cuddles,

and bear-sized cuddles

for being
extra brave.

We give thank you
very much cuddles,
I’m so glad you’re
my friend cuddles,

and no cuddles at all please. Not right now.

There are oops!
you had a fall cuddles,
and we're sorry
you're upset cuddles,

and cuddles to say

hip hip hooray!

We won!

We have lots of snuggly,
huggly couch cuddles,

and tickly, giggly,
wriggly cuddles, and–

Shhhh!

Cuddles that are soft and calm and quiet.

BUGS

There are feeling very tired cuddles, and let's be cozy in bed with teddy cuddles...

With just one more cuddle for

sleep tight and good night.

*For Bea,
a great
cuddler
and a
greater
friend.*

– R. A.

COMPENDIUM
live inspired

With special thanks to the entire Compendium family.

Written by: Ruth Austin
Illustrated by: Clare Owen
Edited by: M.H. Clark
Designed by: Jill Labieniec

Library of Congress Control Number: 2016956462
ISBN: 978-1-943200-49-8

2nd printing. Printed in China with soy inks. A091801002